T H E   G U M B O O T

Geese

A N N E   C A M E R O N
ILLUSTRATED BY JUNE HUBER

HARBOUR PUBLISHING

Some sea walls and breakwaters are made of concrete, some are made of rocks and boulders hauled in huge trucks and dumped, load after load after load, until the barrier is built, the force of the waves is broken and the harbour is calm and safe for boats, even small ones like canoes and kayaks. In Powell River, the breakwater near the pulp mill is made of old naval ships, stripped of all gear and filled with concrete. Everyone calls them the hulks.

One springtime, not as long ago as you might think, a mother Canada goose made her nest in the hulks, laid her eggs and sat on them, watching the barges bring wood chips to the mill, watching the steam and smoke from the huge chimneys pour a stain against the blue sky, watching tugs come and go, watching people arrive for work and leave for home, setting her eggs and waiting for them to hatch.

She sat on her eggs in the daytime, she sat on her eggs at night, she sat on her eggs in the sunshine, she sat on her eggs in the rain. The workers at the mill could see her, sitting patiently and watching the people who watched her. Some-

5

times people went out in motorboats to troll for salmon, and they too saw the goose watching them as they watched her. Sometimes people in kayaks paddled close to the hulks to stare at the goose, and the goose stared at the people in kayaks while they stared at her. Soon everybody watched the goose watch everybody.

One day, a tug brought a string of barges from way, way, way up-coast and parked the barges near the hulks, waiting until their loads of wood chips were needed in the mill. And, on one of the barges, way up on the heap of

chopped-up trees, sat . . . another mother Canada
goose on another nest full of eggs!

And one mother goose watched the other
mother goose. The millworkers watched both
geese, who watched the workers watch them.
One barge after another was moved, the chips
unloaded, the empty barge taken away. Eventually the day came when the barge on which the
second goose had her nest had to be emptied into
the mill.

The workers did not want the mother goose
or her nest to be hurt. They waited until it was
dark and the goose was half asleep, then they
made their way to the barge, to the top of the
heap of chips, and carefully, they moved forward.

A goose will not abandon her eggs, because
she knows her babies are growing inside and if
she leaves them, something awful will happen.

7

The mother goose hissed warning, she spread her wings, she looked as fierce and angry as she could, but the men knew she would not fly away, and they knew she could not hurt them. They moved close enough to throw someone's jacket over her, pin her wings to her sides, hold her head so she could not nip, and then, while one worker carried the goose, the others took the eggs and the nest and moved everything off the pile of chips.

They got in a rowboat and took the enraged goose to the hulks, put her nest near the other nest, put her eggs in the nest, then put her on the eggs, whipped off the jacket and left — quickly.

The mother goose settled onto her eggs and hissed her outrage all night. When the sun came up the next day, she was still warning everybody to stay away, and she was still making threats at

lunchtime. But by suppertime, she had calmed down and only muttered to herself occasionally. The first goose nattered companionably, agreeing with everything the second goose had to say about the eviction and resettlement, and both geese watched as the barge was moved close to the mill, emptied, then taken away. They sat on the two nests on the hulks, watching the comings and goings, watching the people who came to watch them.

And then, one morning there was only one goose on the hulks, one goose but two nests and two piles of eggs. And some scattered feathers.

Things like that happen. Everyone needs to eat. Otters need to eat, seals need to eat, eagles need to eat, raccoons need to eat, and everything eats something else.

The workers saw the feathers and the empty nest and the eggs, and they knew somebody had to do something. So they rowed over to the hulks and moved the cooling eggs from the empty nest to the nest where there was still a mother goose.

9

Nobody could remember if it was the first goose that had gone missing or the second goose, but whichever one was still there, she settled herself over all the eggs, ruffled her feathers, nittered and nattered and onk-onk-onked fretfully until the workers all got back in the rowboat and left her alone with her eggs and her goose-thoughts.

She sat on the hulks on her nest full of eggs, while each day slipped into the other like links on a chain, day-night, day-night, day-night, the way it has always been, back, back, back to that first day when wonder met magic and miracles began to happen, one after the other, each miracle preparing the way for other miracles, each marvel giving birth to other marvels, each priceless, precious thing finding its own place in the togetherness we know as our world.

And one afternoon, eggs began to hatch. Little greenish-coloured goslings came from inside

10

the eggs, opened their eyes, struggled and wriggled and stumbled and peeped. The sun and wind helped dry their feathers, and they stood on their little black feet and peered past their little black beaks. And the very first thing they saw was...MOTHER!

And Mother saw them. It didn't matter to her that some of those baby geese had come out of the other goose's eggs. It didn't matter to her that some of her goslings were adopted. A baby is a baby is a baby, and all of them are just plain wonderful.

The mother goose made soft noises. She made I-love-you noises, she made oh-how-gorgeous noises, she made come-to-me-my-darling noises, she made let's-go-swimming-together noises. And the goslings moved with her off the nest and over the side of the hulk and down into the ocean.

They veed out behind Mother, each of them making little peet-peet-peet noises so she would always know where they were. Peet-peet-peet-peet, they said. Onk-onk-onk, she said. Peet onk peet onk peet onk and off they went to have the adventures of their lives.

Leaving some eggs unhatched in the nest.

"Oh dear," said a worker, "oh dear, oh dear, oh dear." And he got in the rowboat and went over to the hulk, climbed up and carefully, carefully, carefully put the eggs in his pocket, then climbed back down into the rowboat and took the eggs back to the mill. He wrapped the eggs in his sweater, then put the bundle in his lunch kit. Cross-my-fingers'n'make-a-wish, he muttered, just like when he was a little kid, please-please, he hoped, cross-my-fingers'n'make-a-wish.

As soon as his　　　　shift was done, he picked up his lunch bucket and, carrying it very VERY carefully, he walked to his car, his fingers and toes all crossed up, his wish-wish-wish still echoing in his head and his heart. He drove to his friend's place and walked up the steps carrying the lunch kit. He knocked on the door.

"Irvine," he said, "look what I've got here," and he opened his lunch kit.

"You're not supposed to disturb a goose nest!" Irvine scolded. But then, when he heard the story, he nodded. "Right," he said. "Someone had to do something."

Irvine took his friend down to the basement and showed him the incubator where he hatched hen's eggs every year. Together they set the thermostat and plugged in the cord, put in the thermometer so they could check the temperature, put a dish of water inside to make up for the moisture the mother goose makes with her own body. When everything was as right as they could make it, they put the eggs in the warm incubator.

"Wish-wish-wish," said the worker.

"Wish-wish-wish," Irvine agreed.

One day, two days, three days, four, five, six days, and on the seventh morning, when Irvine went down to check, one of the eggs was pipped. By the time the breakfast dishes were done, a little fluffy green gosling was hatched. Irvine put it in a box with some straw, and by lunchtime that gosling had company. By suppertime all the eggs were hatched. Four green-coloured goslings with black feet, black legs, black beaks and black eyes were peet-peet-peeting in the box.

At night, when it was dark, Irvine went out to the henhouse to where a black-and-red banty hen was sitting on her eggs, clucking, clucking, clucking sleepily. "Come on, old girl," Irvine said softly. "Got a job for you to do." He took Hen and her eggs into the house. He put the eggs in the incubator, and he put Hen, still more asleep than awake, in the box with the goslings.

In the morning, when Irvine went down to the basement to check, Hen was all fluffed up and proud. Buuuuck-buck-buck-buck, she crooned. Buuuck, look at my babies! And Hen didn't care that her babies looked like no other babies she had ever hatched in her life, that they were a different colour, a different size, a different shape, or that they said peet-peet instead of cheep-cheep. She had gone to sleep on a pile of eggs and she had wakened surrounded by fuzzy babies.

Irvine opened the basement door, and Hen walked out into the yard with her goslings following

14

her. Choooook-choooook, she said. Peet-peet-peet, they said. "Well, look at that," said Irvine.

When the goslings were two weeks old, Irvine got worried about them. They did not want to stay in the chicken pen. They wanted out on the green, green tender grass, and they found more ways than you would believe to get on the wrong side of the fence. Sometimes Irvine had no idea how the goslings had managed to get out of the pen, but there they were on the lawn, with the neighbourhood dogs going up and down the sidewalks, eyeing them.

So Irvine put Hen and the goslings in a box, put the box in the trunk of his car and drove out of town to a place where two women lived on a stump-ranch—a piece of land with trees and a meadow and a great big pond and different kinds of birds, including Crocus, a Chinese weed-eating gander.

Irvine explained to the women about the hulks, the barge, the two geese, the feathers, the goslings and the eggs. He had a cup of coffee with the women, then had another. And then he took the box containing one irate hen and four very puzzled goslings out of the trunk of the car and put it on the green grass. No sooner was the box open than the hen came out, scolding angrily. Cluck-cluck-cluck-SQUAWK, she said. Peet-peet-peet, the babies agreed.

Hen marched off across the grass, her feathers ruffled, her dignity disturbed, and the goslings followed. "Look," one of the women laughed, "they're wearing gumboots!"

Irvine drove off, and the women watched the goslings as they nipped at the grass and clover. Hen calmed down and stopped scolding the en-

tire world, and all the other creatures on the stump-ranch went back to doing what they did every day. The turkeys did turkey things, and chickens did chicken things, the ducks did duck things, and the dogs behaved the way country dogs are supposed to—they did not chase the goslings or bother the hen. Crocus the Chinese weed-eating gander supervised everything. He walked around, stately and dignified, giving his opinions on everything, keeping one eye peeled for hawks and eagles, and raising a big ruckus if anyone drove into the yard.

That night, Hen went into the fenced yard,
safe from raccoons and mink and owls and all the
creatures that hunt at night, and the goslings
went with her. The country dogs patrolled the
clearing, ready to waken everyone if danger poked
its nose near the stump-ranch.

And in the morning when the women opened the gate in the fence, the hen walked out
with the goslings. The turkeys walked out,
too. And so did the ducks. And the ducks
headed directly for the pond! Splash splash splash,
the water rose in droplets as the ducks had their
bath. The goslings heard the noise and looked.
They did not know what a pond was, they did not
know they were not chickens, they had never
been in water. But they did know that whatever
those ducks were doing, THEY were supposed to
do that, too! They beelined it for the pond and
raced into the water.

Hen went nuts! Cluck-cluuuck-SQUAWK! she screeched. Buck-buck-buckabucka-BUCK, she screeched. But the goslings were at home in the water and could not understand why their mother wouldn't come in with them. The more fun they had, the more hysterical Hen became, until the only thing the women could do was scoop her up, put her in a box and take her back to Irvine's place.

Irvine put Hen in a dark room, where she immediately closed her eyes, tucked her head under her wing and went to sleep, exhausted by all her screeching and squawking. "I'll put chicks in with her tonight," he said, "and she'll be okay by tomorrow."

The women went home, where the goslings were having a wonderful time in the water. Just about the time they began to miss the mother hen and to peet-peet-peet worriedly for her, Crocus the Chinese weed-eating gander decided to have his bath. He stepped into the water, as dignified as any swan, his pearly-grey-and-soft-brown feathers shining in the late afternoon sun. He began to swim regally in the pond. And the goslings noticed Crocus's feet were not black. They were ORANGE.

One gosling ducked his head under the water and nipped at the big orange flappers. Crocus HONKed insult. A second gosling ducked under the water and nipped. Then another. Then the fourth. One after the other they went under the water and had a nibble at the orange flappers, as Crocus gave them goose-lectures about respect, about how some things are just not done, about how goslings should behave in certain ways, especially when dealing with dignified adult ganders.

The goslings did not care. Peet-peet, they said excitedly, peet-peet, orange feet!

Crocus was so appalled that he left the pond in a huff. The goslings followed. Crocus walked away from the pond. The goslings veed out behind him, just as they had veed out behind Hen. Peet-peet-peet, they said, so he would know where they were at all times.

"Go away," Crocus grumped. "Go tell your mother she's calling you."

"But she's not!" said one gosling. "I can't hear her, I can't see her, I don't know where she is."

"You have orange feet," said a second gosling.

"Mother had orange feet," said a third gosling.

"I think YOU are Mother," said the fourth gosling.

"NO!" Crocus protested.

"Yes!" the goslings all agreed. "Mother had orange feet, you have orange feet. You are Mother."

Crocus spent the rest of the day trying to stay six feet ahead of the goslings. The goslings spent the rest of the day trying to keep up with Crocus.

At night, the women put all the birds in the big fenced yard, and Crocus settled himself for sleep. Peet-peet-peet, the goslings said sadly. "No mum, no mum, no mum, peet-peet-peet, it's dark and I'm scared!"

They peet-peet-peeted so sadly, huddled to-gether for comfort in a world gone dark and cold, that Crocus could not stand it. He just could—not—stand it. A lonely baby is a lonely baby is a lonely baby, and when a gander is a father, he helps care for the goslings just as much as the mother goose does.

"Be quiet," Crocus said softly. "There is no need for you to feel frightened. We are safe behind this fence, the dogs are on guard, the dark is not a bad thing, it is just the soft velvet dark.

And anyway, there are stars in the sky and a moon will appear soon."

"But it's cold," one peet-peet-peeted, not at all convinced. "My head is cold, my beak is cold, my body is cold and my black feet are cold!"

"It is not cold," Crocus quarrelled. "I am not cold! Not cold at all."

"Let me see," a gosling blurted. And — ZIP! — like that, one of the goslings was snuggled up against Crocus. And then another. And another, and the last, all of them huddled up against Crocus, all of them going peet-peet-peet.

"Hush now," Crocus muffed, arching his neck and using his black beak to push a gosling farther under his wing. "Hush, now. Go to sleep."

"I'm not sleepy," the stubborn one insisted.

"When I was a gosling," Crocus said, "and I could not get to sleep, my mother would tell me to count the stars. And I never once got past six million and ten. See if you can. One...two... three...four..."

Soon all the goslings were asleep, and Crocus sighed a huge sigh of relief. He had not intended to get into parenting. He especially had not intended to get into parenting four black-billed, green-tinged goslings who looked as if they were strutting around wearing black gumboots! But a baby is a baby is a baby, and Crocus was a gander, and if you are not a mother and not a father, chances are you are an uncle, unless you happen to be an aunt.

In the morning, as soon as the gate in the fence was opened, Crocus headed out with his gaggle of goslings. Straight for the pond they went! Splash, splash and splash.

"Orange feet!" they yelled, diving down and biting Crocus's toes.

"Here, here, you," Crocus scolded. He dove under the water. "Black beaks," he teased, grabbing a gosling beak and tugging ever so gently. "Black toes black toes nip nip so it goes."

"Orange feet orange toes nip nip so it goes," they agreed.

Crocus and the goslings swam and dove, they raced and chased, they nipped and played until the top of the pond was whipped to a froth and the ducks stood on the shore and watched, amazed. "Goose goings-on, I suppose," said the fat old duck. "Goose goings-on," the others agreed, bobbing their heads and waiting for the rowdies to get out of the pond and allow the dignified their turns.

Eventually, the geese came out of the pond and started in on the grass and clover. Every day, all day, except for a nap in the afternoon, they spent their time eating grass and clover and watercress, swimming and diving, toe-nipping and froth-making. Day after day, sunny or rainy, Crocus with his orange feet and legs and the goslings with their black gumboots went up and down in the clearing, back and forth to the pond, and bit by bit, feather by feather, the goslings lost their greenish down and began to look like what they were, Canada geese. They grew and grew and grew and grew but they never did grow necks as long and curvy as Crocus's, so they never looked quite as big as he did, even though they were heavier than he was, and they never looked as graceful.

Several times during the summer, grandchildren arrived to visit the women, and one of the first things the kids did was to get slices of bread and hurry outside to break the bread into small pieces and feed them to the geese. "Ah," said Crocus contentedly, "grandchildren! Grandchildren and bread!" He arched his neck and preened his feathers and looked as beautiful as he could look. He didn't even run away when the grandchildren stroked his feathers or touched his head — not even when they put their arms around him and cuddled him.

"Not me," said one of the young Canada geese. "Not me!" And no matter how crafty the grandchildren were, they did not get close enough to cuddle any of the young geese.

Summer passed and the leaves began to fall from the trees. The days got shorter, the nights got longer, and one evening a positively gigantic vee of Canada geese winged across the sky. Honk-honk-honk-honk-honk-honk-honk, they called, honk-honk heading south honk-honk migration time honk-honk off we go honk-honk beware the snow!

"What are they?" asked one young goose.

"Honkers," Crocus said wisely. "Every year at this time, they fly south."

"Why?" asked another young goose.

"As the weather turns," Crocus replied, "there is less light, and without the light they cannot find enough food here. So they go south, where the days are longer and there is lots of food. In the spring, they fly north again."

"We have lots of food," the nit-picky young debater said. "Every morning and every evening those women come out and put grain where we can get it. Why don't the honkers come here and eat grain?"

"I don't know," Crocus said. "I've often wondered that myself."

27

"Such a strange way to do things," said the fourth gosling, cuddling against Uncle Crocus, settling himself for the night. None of them knew that if things had happened in a different way, they too would be part of a southwarding vee, with a mom and a dad to teach them how to survive the long journey.

Every day for a week or more, vee after vee after vee of Canada geese headed south. Sometimes snow geese travelled with them. Morning, afternoon, evening, even at night the honkers headed south, honk-honk-honk-honk, and one night everyone in the barnyard watched as the honkers veed across the face of the moon.

The next morning, they were in the pond, just paddling around catching their breath after a great game of orange-feet-black-feet, when they heard one thready, weak voice calling honk... honk...honk... One lone, weak, thready voice flying below the level of the trees, circling the clearing. Honk...honk...honk...

HONK-HONK-HONK! the young geese called. HONK-HONK-HONK!

And then, down the driveway, feet hanging, wings flapping, the lone little wild Canada goose came.

The two women stood in the driveway, eyes wide, watching. Down, down, down, like an airplane coming in for a landing, feet hanging the way plane wheels hang, down, down, down the driveway, across the clearing and—SPLASH!—into the pond.

The migrating goose sat in the water in the middle of the pond, so tired she could hardly move her feet. And one after the other, with no pushing or shoving or silliness, one at a time the tame Canada geese moved forward.

"Look," one of the women breathed, "they're introducing themselves."

"One by one," the other woman agreed. "And so politely!"

One by one, one at a time, one after the other, the tame Canada geese swam forward and bobbed heads. They touched beaks with the wild Canada goose. They made little nittery noises, and then they all swam around her in an excited circle, splashing and celebrating, each and every one of them very very VERY happy that a wild goose had come to call.

Twice around the pond they went with the wild goose, quiet in the middle of the splash. Then she joined the chase, and all five of them went around the pond, splash splash, with Uncle Crocus chortling from the bank, watching his charges behave in a proper fashion.

And when they had explored the possibilities
of the pond, they came from the water, one after
the other, with the wild goose at the very end,
watching to see how things were done in this part
of the great and wonderful world.

"See," the tame geese said proudly, "we have
grass. We have all the grass we need. Please eat
some grass, we have more than enough." "See,"
they said. "We have clover, we have lots of clover,
we have all the clover we need, please help your-
self."

The wild goose began to eat, and it was obvi-
ous from the very start that she was about as
hungry as any tired goose could be.

"Oh my dear," said one woman, "oh, she is so
thin! She is so hungry! Why, she is STARVING!"

"I'll put out some grain," said the other woman.
She went to the big green barrel where the grain
was kept, got a big can full of grain and spread it
on the ground.

"She doesn't know what it is."

"Oh the poor thing," the other agreed. "She is so thin! She is so tired! Look, her little black gumboot legs are shaking! Oh, I wonder what went wrong for her."

"Sometimes something happens. A fox, maybe, or an owl. And the first clutch of eggs is eaten. And so the mother and father goose make another nest, and they try again. But that means the goslings hatch late, and THAT means they don't have as much time to grow big and strong. Which would mean..."

"Which would mean that when it came time for them to migrate, they might not be able to keep up..."

"And if they couldn't keep up, they might get lost..."

"And then..."

"Oh, poor little thing!" they both said.

The tame geese showed the wild goose all the good things in the clearing. They showed her the

clover, they showed her the grass, they showed her the watercress, and she tried it all, eating as fast as she could. "This is grain," they said repeatedly. "See, if you eat this, you'll feel better." And finally, the wild goose tried the grain.

"Ah," the women sighed with relief. "That will do her a world of good!"

"Look," said one. "She is much much MUCH smaller than our geese."

"Maybe she is a sub-species," the other said. "There are many sub-species of Canada geese. Big Canada geese, small Canada geese, and yet they are all Canada geese."

"Just like people! Some of us are tall and some of us are short, some of us are skinny and some of us are chubby, some of us have blond hair, some of us have brown hair, some have black hair or red hair or pale skin or dark skin or straight hair or curly hair. But we are all people."

Both women expected the wild goose to fill up on food and then leave. Instead, when night began to fall and the women closed the birds up safe behind the fence, there were five Canada geese clustered around Crocus.

"Nice to have a visitor," Crocus said politely.

"She is our wild cousin from the North," one of the young geese said proudly.

"She has seen WONDERFUL things," another young goose bragged excitedly. "She has seen—are you ready for this, Uncle Crocus?—she has seen the NORTHERN LIGHTS!"

"The what?" Crocus asked.

The wild goose explained all about them. Crocus listened, nodding his head to show he understood, even if her accent was a bit different from his.

In the morning, when the women opened the gate, Crocus led the way out of the yard, followed by four big fine fat tame Canada geese and one smaller, very thin and still extremely hungry wild Canada goose. When the women spread grain, the wild goose knew just as well as the tame ones what to do with it.

Day after day, as the weather got colder, the wild goose visited with her tame cousins. Long night after long night, she told stories of the North and of all the things she had seen. In turn, the tame geese told their stories, and Crocus shared all the things he had seen in his long life. He told of fall fairs and poultry shows, where he went in a travel cage and stood proudly while the judges looked him over, announced he was as fine a Chinese weed-eating gander as they had ever seen, then pinned ribbons to his cage. He told of rides down the highway in the back of a pick-up truck, and of one place he had lived where a small boy rode his tricycle up and down the driveway while Crocus ran beside him, enjoying every minute.

When the snow fell and the pond froze, the geese did not mind at all. They had plenty of grain and their feathers insulated them, so they stayed warm and fat. At Christmas time and again at spring break, the grandchildren came to visit. They broke slices of bread into small pieces and tossed them to the geese, who clustered happily around the wonderful bits and crumbs, eating both the crusts and the soft centres. "Oh my," the wild Canada goose said. "Oh my, this is almost as good as watching the Northern Lights!"

And then it was springtime. Pussywillows showed their faces in the brush around the pond, daffodils began to yellow-up around the house, and overhead the wild honkers headed north in large vees.

One morning, the wild cousin from the North could not resist the honk-honk-honk of the migrating geese, and she flew up, up, up, heading down the driveway, up up up up and off with the wild geese, honking her thanks and her farewell.

The two women stood watching, and one of them wiped tears from her eyes. "Oh," she said, "I do hope she remembers what they taught her about hunters. And foxes. And wolves. And... the world is full of danger, you know. It is full of marvels and mystery, it is full of miracle and wonder, but it is also full of danger."

The tame geese honked and honked and honked, but the wild cousin did not come back.

"You must not try to talk her into a life she does not want," Crocus said gently. "She has seen the Northern Lights, remember. She has seen the barren lands and the cold Arctic sea. That is her life, and she has the right to choose."

"But I MISS her!" the debater whined.

Crocus nodded his head. "So do I."

Spring moved gently across the land. The chickens sat on their clutches of eggs and hatched out broods of fluffy yellow fuzz-balls, the birds nested in the trees and soon were busy taking berries and bugs to their babies. The women worked in the garden, planting new crops of lettuce and tomatoes and beans.

Each day was longer than the one before it, each day was warmer, and then it was summertime. The grass grew, the clover grew, the watercress grew, and there was grain every morning and every evening. The grandchildren came for their holidays and broke slices of bread into little pieces, then fed the pieces to the tame Canada geese and to Crocus, who did not mind when they cuddled him and hugged him. The tame geese still were not up for that kind of familiarity, and they made sure there was always at least eight feet between them and any child.

The world turned again in the way it has done since the very first day, and soon summer was fading, and autumn was moving in for her visit. The leaves on the trees began to change colour and drift to the ground. One morning there was frost on the clover. The vees of migrating geese passed overhead, long long arms of vees, each goose knowing his or her exact place in the vee, honk-hoonnk-hoooonnnkkkk across the face of the moon.

And one day, honk-honk-honk, down the driveway, feet hanging, like a plane coming in for a landing, the north-ern cousin returned! Honk-honk-honk! she called. HONK-HONK-HONK! Following her were SIX young wild Canada geese, and bringing up the rear was their guardian and protector, a wild Canada gander, HONK-HONK.

"Visitors!" the tame geese celebrated.

"My word," Crocus said to himself. "Eight of them! One last year, eight this year, one can hardly bring oneself to wonder what will arrive next year."

"Look, look, look look LOOK!" the women shouted. "Oh, LOOOOOOK! Quick! Let's phone Irvine! Phone the grandchildren!"

"Put some grain out for them," Crocus grumbled. And even though he grumbled in goose, the women must have under-stood because they turned and raced up to the shed where the big green barrel was kept. They brought grain and spread it on the grass.

"Try this," the tame geese invited their wild cousins. "It's very good. It will make you feel much better."

"Are you sure, my dear?" asked the wild Canada gander. "Really sure?"

"Oh, quite sure," the wild Canada goose said happily. "There is no need for all that flying and dodging hunters with guns and being blown around by storms and such things as you told me about. There is grain here all through the cold time. We can go behind the fence at night, safe from all manner of predator. And in the spring, when the others head North, why, we can just go with them. If we choose," she added.

"I," said one young wild goose, tasting grain for the first time in her life, "could get very used to this."

"Wait until the grandchildren come to visit," said Crocus, "and you get to taste bread!"

"Ah, yes, bread," the wild Canada goose said. "Bread! You have no idea how many times I have wished for bread. I missed it as much as I missed the Northern Lights when I was down here!"

ANNE CAMERON, one of Canada's best-loved writers, was born in Nanaimo, BC. She learned the art of storytelling from Scottish, English, Native and Chinese storytellers in her community, and has been writing nearly all her life. She is the author of many books of fiction and poetry, and she writes regularly for radio, stage and screen. Her children's books of native Indian legends have become steady bestsellers throughout North America.

JUNE HUBER was born on Vancouver Island and remains a true West Coaster. Her watercolours recreate coastal scenes, yet are injected with her own unique imagery. Though largely self-taught, she has had several one-woman shows in British Columbia plus numerous inclusions in group shows across Canada. She now teaches art at Malaspina College in Powell River, BC. She is the mother of four children and lives in Lund, near Powell River. This is her first book.

HARBOUR PUBLISHING
P.O. Box 219
Madeira Park, BC Canada V0N 2H0

Fourth Printing, 2000

Canadian Cataloguing in Publication Data

Cameron, Anne, 1938–
  The gumboot geese

  ISBN 1-55017-063-5

  I. Huber, June.   II. Title.
PS8555.A5187G8 1992   jC813'.54   C92-091164-1
PZ7.C35Gu 1992

Published with the assistance of the Canada Council and the British
Columbia Cultural Services Branch
Jacket and interior design by Roger Handling
Typeset in Elante
Printed and bound in Canada by Friesen Printers